Poppy the Posh Kitten

Looking through the window of the cat basket, Poppy stared at the tiny house in front of her. She couldn't help feeling shocked. *This* was where she was going to live? What would Princess say if she saw it? The Siamese had told her that all pedigree cats lived in big houses . . .

Bob the Bouncy Kitten

"In you go, Bob," Amy said. She lowered the wriggling ginger bundle into the basket. Bob twitched and squirmed and made mewing noises of protest. "Shut the lid, Mum!"

From the basket, Bob looked up at them, his eyes dark and wide. Then, just as the lid was almost closed, he made a leap for freedom. Squeezing himself out of a tiny opening, he bounced onto the carpet and raced across the room.

Titles in Jenny Dale's KITTEN TALES™ series

Star the Snowy Kitten
Felix the Fluffy Kitten
Nell the Naughty Kitten
Patch the Perfect Kitten
Lucy the Lonely Kitten
Snuggles the Sleepy Kitten
Pip the Prize Kitten
Sid the Speedy Kitten

Jenny Dale's KITTEN TALES books can
be ordered from the Pan Macmillan website,
www.panmacmillan.com, or from your local book-
shop and are also available by post from:

Bookpost, PO Box 29, Douglas,
Isle of Man IM99 1BQ
(tel: 01624 836000
email: bookshop@enterprise.net
www.bookpost.co.uk)

Jenny Dale's KITTEN TALES™

A Kitten Tales Two-Books-in-One Special!

Poppy the Posh Kitten
Bob the Bouncy Kitten

by Jenny Dale

Illustrated by Susan Hellard

A Working Partners Book

MACMILLAN CHILDREN'S BOOKS

Poppy the Posh Kitten first published 2001 by Macmillan Children's Books

Bob the Bouncy Kitten first published 1999 by Macmillan Children's Books
a division of Macmillan Publishers Limited
20 New Wharf Road, London N1 9RR
Basingstoke and Oxford
www.panmacmillan.com

Associated companies throughout the world

Created by Working Partners Limited
London W6 0QT

ISBN 0 330 43283 4

Text copyright © Working Partners 1999, 2001
Illustrations copyright © Susan Hellard 1999, 2001
Kitten Tales is a trademark of Working Partners Limited

3 5 7 9 8 6 4 2

A CIP catalogue record for this book is available from
the British Library.

Typeset by SX Composing DTP, Rayleigh, Essex
Printed and bound in Great Britain by Mackays of Chatham plc, Kent

Poppy the Posh Kitten

Special thanks to Narinder Dhami

Chapter One

"Poppy! What are you doing?"
Poppy jumped guiltily at the
sound of Princess's sharp miaow.
She wasn't doing *anything*, really.
She was out in the huge garden,
in the run which had been
specially built for Mrs Kent's cats.
Poppy was longing to explore the

1

rest of the garden. She'd been poking at the wire mesh with her paw to see if she could make a hole in it and get through.

"You were trying to get out of the run, weren't you?" Princess, a cream-and-chocolate-coloured Siamese cat, strolled down the run towards Poppy. Her blue eyes were fixed accusingly on the fluffy white kitten.

"No, I wasn't, Princess!" Poppy mewed. Princess was very beautiful, with her silky coat and sparkling eyes. Even though she was a little scared of the bigger cat, Poppy hoped she would be just as beautiful when she grew up. Mrs Kent owned five show cats, including Poppy's mum,

Dorcas. But none of the cats had won as many cups, medals and rosettes as Princess.

"You *are* silly, Poppy," Princess sniffed, looking the kitten up and down. "Why on earth do you want to get out of the run? You're safe in here."

"I just wanted to have a look

around," Poppy miaowed.

"What, and meet some of those dirty, common cats who come into the garden sometimes?" Princess snapped. She sounded quite alarmed at the thought. "Just remember you're a *pedigree* cat, Poppy. A pedigree cat mustn't have anything to do with common old moggies – they're not as beautiful or as clever as us!"

"Yes, Princess," Poppy mewed obediently.

"You don't want to be like one of *those* cats," Princess went on, holding her chocolate-coloured nose in the air. "They live in tiny houses, not lovely big ones like Mrs Kent's, and they have to eat food out of *tins*!" She shuddered.

"It's disgusting!"

Poppy copied Princess and looked disgusted too. Dorcas was always telling Poppy that Princess was snooty, and not to take any notice of her. But Poppy couldn't help it. The Siamese was *so* beautiful, and she'd won *so* many competitions. Poppy wanted to be just like her.

"Those cats run about and climb trees and get all mussed up," Princess went on. She stretched out one leg, and delicately cleaned her toes. "And their owners don't care a bit! But *pedigree* owners like us to be clean and beautiful all the time, because they care about us so much."

Just then, Mrs Kent appeared at

the top of the run. "Poppy! Princess!" she called. "Dinner!"

"Oh, good," purred Princess. She walked off towards the house, her long tail swishing from side to side. "I hope it's fresh fish today."

Poppy ran after her, licking her lips. When she reached the kitchen, Mrs Kent was putting down five bowls of fish on the floor. Poppy went and tucked into the bowl next to her mum's.

"I hope that Princess hasn't been putting silly ideas into your head, Poppy," miaowed Dorcas in between mouthfuls.

"No, Mum," Poppy mewed back. But as she ate, Poppy thought about all those poor cats who had to eat horrible food that came in tins. Yuck! She couldn't help feeling sorry for them, even though Princess said that they were common. *I hope I don't ever have to eat tinned food*, Poppy thought to herself. It sounded *awful*!

"I'm going to brush you now, Poppy," Mrs Kent said, when the kitten had cleaned her bowl. "Up you come."

Poppy began to purr. She loved being brushed and groomed. The brush tickled and it left her fur all fluffy and soft. She had never been dirty in her life.

"Only common old moggies get dirty," Princess had told Poppy.

And since then, Poppy had

done her very best to keep her
thick, long-haired fur clean and
beautiful.

"I've got a surprise for you,
Poppy," Mrs Kent went on, as she
brushed Poppy's already
gleaming coat. "Lisa and her
mum are coming to visit today."

Poppy's big blue eyes lit up. She
loved Mrs Kent's granddaughter,

Lisa. Whenever Lisa came over, they always played lots of games together. And Lisa would brush Poppy's coat until she looked like a fluffy white cloud. "Brilliant!" she purred.

Just then, the doorbell rang. Poppy jumped off Mrs Kent's lap. "Is that Lisa now?" she miaowed excitedly. "Open the door, Mrs Kent!"

Mrs Kent went down the hall to the front door, and Poppy dashed after her. At least, Poppy was *going* to dash after her until she spotted Princess eyeing her sternly.

"Pedigree cats don't charge around all over the place like common old moggies do!"

Princess had told Poppy firmly.

So Poppy trotted calmly and coolly down the hall after Mrs Kent, even though she was so excited to see Lisa.

"Hello, Gran," said Lisa. She hurried in, followed by her mum, Mrs Martin. "Hello, Poppy!" And she picked the kitten up.

Poppy was already purring like an engine. She rubbed her head happily against Lisa's cheek.

"Have you told Poppy yet, Gran?" Lisa asked excitedly.

"Told me what?" Poppy miaowed, puzzled.

"You're coming to live with me and Mum and Barney today, Poppy!" Lisa announced, her eyes shining. "You're going to be *my*

kitten! Isn't that brilliant?"

"Oh!" Poppy mewed. She'd known, of course, that one day she'd have to leave Mrs Kent's, and go to a new home. But she'd never *dreamed* she'd be going to live with Lisa!

Mrs Kent turned to Lisa's mum with a smile. "I'm glad that you finally agreed to let Lisa have

Poppy," she said.

Mrs Martin laughed. "Well, as you know, we've already got Barney, and I thought two cats would be too much. But Lisa loves Poppy so much, I couldn't keep saying no!"

Mrs Kent nodded. "Yes, I know Poppy will be going to a good home," she said, stroking the kitten's fluffy head. "You *will* remember to brush her every day, won't you, Lisa?"

"Of course I will!" Lisa said.

"Don't worry, Lisa," Poppy mewed. "I'll make sure I stay clean and beautiful!"

Some of the other cats came over to see what was going on.

"So, my little Poppy is going to

a new home?" purred Dorcas, wrapping herself around Lisa's ankles.

Poppy looked down at her mum from Lisa's arms. "Yes, Mum!" she mewed. "I'll miss you, but isn't it exciting?"

Princess sat in the doorway, delicately washing her face with a chocolate-brown paw. "I bet your new home won't be as nice as this one!" she purred smugly.

"Don't you listen, Poppy," Dorcas miaowed firmly. "You'll be fine with Lisa."

Princess sniffed. "Well, just you remember all the things I've taught you, Poppy," she purred snootily. "You're a pedigree cat, and don't you forget it!"

Chapter Two

"Here we are, Poppy." Lisa lifted up the cat basket so that the kitten could see out of the car window. "This is your new home!"

Looking through the basket's window, Poppy stared at the tiny house in front of her. She couldn't help feeling shocked. *This* was where she was going to live? What would Princess say if she saw it? The Siamese had told her that all pedigree cats lived in big houses, like Mrs Kent's!

Poppy felt rather gloomy as Lisa carried her up the path to the front door. But she cheered up a bit when they went inside. Even though the house was small, it was warm and cosy. *Maybe it won't be too bad*, she told herself. *After all, even if the house is tiny, I'll be able to run around outside.*

Lisa put the cat basket down on the kitchen floor, then opened it. "Come on out, Poppy," she said happily.

Poppy stepped delicately out of

the basket and took a good look around. There was a cat flap in the back door, just like she was used to. The one at Mrs Kent's house led to the large run that all the cats played in. Poppy padded over to the door, and gave the flap a push with her head.

It didn't move.

"The cat flap's locked, Poppy," Lisa said. "You can't go out into the garden until you've had your injections."

Poppy looked up at Lisa, feeling puzzled. "Haven't you got a special run for me?" she mewed.

But as she stared through the clear plastic window in the cat flap, Poppy saw that the Martins' garden wasn't like Mrs Kent's at all. Lisa's gran had neat lawns and flowerbeds. This garden had long grass – some of it was taller than Poppy! And bushes, and big, shadowy trees . . .

Suddenly, a furry face looked right back at Poppy from the other side of the cat flap window! Poppy yowled with fright then rushed over to Lisa and ran up her jeans, into her arms. "Save, me, Lisa!" she mewed.

"Ow, ow!" Lisa cried, half laughing. "Poppy! It's OK! It's only Barney," she said, stroking the scared kitten.

"I'll let him in," said Mrs Martin, and she hurried over to the cat flap. She unlocked it and, at once, a young black-and-white tomcat tumbled through it.

"Hi," Barney miaowed, beaming up at Poppy. "I'm Barney! Who are you?"

Poppy, who was still clinging onto Lisa, stared down at Barney. He was *filthy*! His coat was more like black and grey than black and white! And he had leaves and bits of grass stuck to his coat as well! Poppy couldn't imagine what on *earth* Barney must have been doing to get in such a mess. He *did* look friendly though . . .

Seeing that her new kitten was no longer so nervous, Lisa put Poppy back down on the floor.

Barney came over to give Poppy a friendly sniff.

Poppy remembered what Princess had said. "I'm Poppy, the pedigree kitten," she mewed. "And *you* are not very clean!"

"Well, I've been playing outside," Barney miaowed cheerfully. "I can show you all the best places to play in the garden!"

"No, thank you," Poppy mewed snootily, putting her nose in the air just like Princess did.

Barney looked surprised. "Well, if you haven't had your injections yet, we can play in the house instead—"

"I don't *want* to play with you," Poppy hissed. Princess would be very proud of her, she thought. But even so, Poppy couldn't help feeling a bit guilty. Barney was only trying to be friendly.

Barney looked surprised. "Suit yourself," he miaowed. Then his green eyes lit up as Lisa went over to one of the cupboards. "Oh, great – food!"

Poppy was feeling a bit peckish herself. So she trotted over to Lisa too. "Fresh fish is my favourite, Lisa," she mewed hungrily. "And I don't mind chicken, liver and steak too."

But what was that in Lisa's hand? Poppy could hardly believe her eyes. It was a *tin* – a tin of catfood!

"Mmm, that smells good!" purred Barney, as Lisa spooned some of the catfood into two bowls, then put them both on the kitchen floor. "Come on, Poppy – dig in."

"I can't eat *that*!" Poppy squeaked in dismay. She watched Barney begin to eat from one of the bowls. Then her tiny nose twitched in surprise. The food smelled quite nice. But what *would* Princess say if she knew that Poppy had been eating tinned food? She'd never speak to Poppy again!

"Oh well," snuffled Barney. "Can't let it go to waste." And he scoffed Poppy's bowlful as well as his own.

"Aren't you hungry, Poppy?" Lisa asked.

"Yes, I am," Poppy mewed miserably. "But I can't eat that

stuff. You'll have to give me some *proper* food!"

Barney trotted over to the cat flap. "Sure you don't want me to stay in and play with you?" he miaowed.

"Quite sure, thank you," Poppy mewed frostily.

Mrs Martin let Barney out again, and he disappeared into the overgrown garden.

Lisa picked Poppy up. "You'll soon settle in and get used to everything, Poppy," she said kindly, smoothing the kitten's fluffy coat.

Feeling more cheerful, Poppy snuggled down in Lisa's arms. She just had to remember that she was a special, pedigree cat, not a common moggy like Barney. And as long as she kept her coat clean and white and beautiful, everyone would be very proud of her.

Chapter Three

"*Barney*!" Poppy hissed crossly.
"Get away from me!"

The black-and-white cat had just
leaped out at Poppy from behind
the TV. Her tail twitched angrily.
Barney was just too rough!

Barney looked disappointed.
"Come on, let's fight!" he

miaowed. "I won't hurt you."

"No, thank you," Poppy sniffed. She padded out of the living room, her nose in the air.

Poppy had been living with Lisa and Mrs Martin for a week now. And Barney was *always* trying to get her to play with him. How on earth was she supposed to keep her fluffy white coat nice and clean when Barney was such a nuisance? Poppy had decided to eat the tinned food, because there was nothing else, after all. But she was not going to get all dusty and dirty like Barney – no way!

Barney bounded after Poppy, playfully swiping at her plumy tail with his paw. "Where did Lisa take you this morning after breakfast?" he asked curiously.

"To the vet," Poppy mewed gloomily. "He stuck a needle in my neck, and it hurt!"

"Well, that means you've had all your injections. Now you'll be able to come and play outside!" Barney replied. He launched himself at her again. But Poppy side-stepped neatly, and Barney ended up in a tangled black-and-white heap on the hall rug.

"*Outside*?" Poppy repeated, her big blue eyes opening wide. She had forgotten all about that! She hurried over to the back door and stared through the cat flap window, her heart beating fast.

Lisa's garden looked very exciting. There were lots of places to explore, and lots of trees to climb, and—

A pedigree cat doesn't run about or climb trees . . . Poppy could hear Princess's snooty miaow again.

Poppy sat down and began to wash her paws – even though they didn't really need it. *What was I thinking of*? she asked herself glumly. Of course she wouldn't be able to do all those things. She had to keep herself clean and tidy, or Lisa wouldn't be proud of her any more. Princess had said that pedigree owners liked their cats to look beautiful all the time.

But to Poppy's surprise, Lisa came into the kitchen and opened the door. "Guess what, Poppy," she said. "We're going out to play in the garden!"

"Told you, Pops!" Barney miaowed eagerly. He shot out into the garden, calling, "Come on!"

Poppy sniffed. "I won't be going outside *that* much," she mewed. "And *don't* call me Pops!"

But standing in the doorway, Poppy couldn't help feeling excited. The interesting new smells made her whiskers twitch. She followed Lisa outside, onto the little patio. Her blue eyes darted from side to side.

The garden seemed much bigger now that Poppy was in it. The overgrown lawn was dotted with yellow flowers and filled with buzzing bees and fluttering butterflies. At the bottom of the garden, where the trees grew close together, the grass was very long. It looked really exciting.

"Go on, Poppy," Lisa said. "Go and explore."

Her heart beating fast, Poppy stepped carefully across the patio, towards the lawn. Then suddenly, Barney popped out from behind a bush and made her jump.

"Barney!" Poppy hissed, her fur all ruffled. Then she stared at the black-and-white cat. He had grass seeds and bits of leaves stuck in his furry coat already.

Poppy stayed where she was – it was nice and clean.

"OK, we'll have a game here then," said Lisa. She took a little rubber ball out of her pocket, and rolled it along the patio.

Poppy knew this game. It was one she could play, and still stay tidy! She chased after the ball, and stopped it with her paw.

"Good girl!" Lisa smiled, and Poppy felt very pleased with

herself. But she couldn't help
sneaking a look at Barney. He was
romping through the long grass,
chasing butterflies. He was
having a great time.

"Well, so am I!" Poppy told
herself firmly.

Then Lisa rolled the ball a bit
too hard. It went off the patio and

into the long grass.

"I can't get that, Lisa," Poppy mewed sadly. "I'll get all messy!"

"I'll get it, Poppy," Lisa called. She went off to find the ball.

Barney was now rolling over and over on the path, stretching himself in the sun, and getting dustier and dirtier. "Come and have a roll on the path, Poppy!" he purred loudly. "It feels great!"

"You must be joking," Poppy mewed snootily. "Look how dirty you are!" But she couldn't help thinking that Barney was having a *much* better time than she was.

Chapter Four

"Shall I or shan't I?" Poppy
mewed to herself, as she sat in
front of the cat flap. It was open
all day now that Poppy had had
her injections. But Poppy hadn't
been out by herself yet.

Poppy was bored. It was
Monday afternoon, so Lisa was at

school and Mrs Martin was at work. Barney had been out in the garden all day because the sun was shining. Not that she cared *where* Barney was, Poppy told herself firmly. But it *was* a bit lonely in the house with no one else there.

Poppy took a deep breath, and began to climb through the flap. Next moment, she was outside on the sunny patio. "I did it!" she miaowed proudly.

"Hey, look at that!" someone called. "What is it?"

Poppy looked round sharply. Three cats were sitting in a row on top of the fence, looking down at her, their tails swinging. One of them was Barney, but Poppy hadn't seen the other two before. One was a big ginger tom, and the other was a small tabby.

"I beg your pardon," Poppy mewed sniffily, "but were you talking to *me*?"

"Oh, it's a *real* cat!" the ginger tom howled to his friends. "I thought it was a cuddly toy!"

"She looks snooty," the smaller tabby miaowed disapprovingly.

"Leave her alone, you two," warned Barney. "Poppy, this is Henry and this is Lily. They're mates of mine."

"I might have known," Poppy sniffed. She sat down on the patio with her back to them, her tail twitching crossly.

"She thinks she's too good for *us*!" Henry miaowed. The three cats jumped down from the fence. "She's Poppy the *Posh* Kitten!"

"Those pedigree cats always think they're better than us," Lily spat.

"Poppy's OK," Barney miaowed. "Come on, let's play Catch-the-Leaf!"

Poppy couldn't help sneaking a quick look. Barney, Henry and Lily were running around in the long grass. It looked like they were having loads of fun as they pounced and leaped around in the sunshine.

Suddenly, Princess's miaow popped into Poppy's mind . . . *A pedigree cat mustn't have anything*

to do with common old moggies!
*They're not as beautiful or as clever
as* we *are!*

No, but they have a lot more fun!
Poppy thought gloomily, as
Barney, Henry and Lily flopped
down on the path and began to
roll around in the dust.

"What shall we do now?"
Barney panted.

"Let's climb one of the trees,"
Henry suggested. "Let's see who
can climb right up to that big
branch over there!"

Poppy looked at the tree Henry
was talking about. It was one of
the tallest in the garden. The big
branch was about halfway up.
It looked almost impossible to
get to.

"What are *you* looking at, Poppy the Posh?" Henry miaowed rudely. "Are *you* going to have a go?"

"Pedigree cats are useless at climbing!" Lily sniffed scornfully.

Suddenly Poppy was fed up with everyone telling her what she couldn't do. She was fed up with sitting on the patio and keeping clean and neat. And most of all, she was fed up with being Poppy the Posh Kitten!

"I *can* climb up there!" she mewed loudly. "In fact, I'll climb up there right now!"

Chapter Five

Poppy hadn't meant to say that at all. In fact, she was even more shocked by what she'd just said than Barney, Henry and Lily were. The three cats sat staring at her, their eyes as round as marbles.

"You don't mean that, Poppy!"

Barney miaowed. He sounded a bit worried.

"'Course she doesn't," Lily scoffed. "She's just showing off."

"As if Poppy the Posh Kitten could climb up there," Henry added. "She couldn't even climb onto a chair!"

"Right!" Her tail ramrod straight, Poppy marched furiously across the patio, and onto the grass. She headed for the tree and stopped at the bottom of it. "Now you'll see whether pedigree cats can climb or not!"

"This should be fun!" Henry remarked. He settled himself down on the path and tucked his paws underneath him.

Poppy looked up at the tree and

gulped. It was *very* high. And she
didn't even know how to start.
Her heart sank. She'd made a fool
of herself in front of Barney and
his friends.

"If you climb up that little tree
there, you can get onto the fence."
Barney was suddenly beside her,
whispering in her ear. "Then
you'll be able to get into the

lower branches of the big tree."

"Thanks," Poppy mewed.

"Take it slowly and don't look down," Barney went on, giving her a gentle nudge. "It's not as difficult as it looks. Good luck!"

Knowing that Barney thought she could do it made Poppy feel a bit braver. She took a deep breath, and set off up the little tree towards the fence.

Climbing the little tree was difficult enough. It swayed in the breeze, and Poppy swayed with it. But she clung on tightly with her claws. And soon, to her delight, she was scrambling onto the top of the fence. She'd done it!

"Well done, Poppy!" Barney miaowed, as she padded carefully

along the fence towards the lowest branches of the big tree.

"Huh! That was nothing," Henry said scornfully. "That was the *easy* bit!"

But Poppy wasn't going to stop now. The big tree didn't look *quite* so big now that she was on top of the fence. And the branch didn't look quite so high.

She set off along the lower branches, placing her paws carefully and delicately as she made her way up the tree. Poppy had never dreamed that she might be good at climbing. But because she was very sure-footed she was doing rather well.

"I'm good at climbing!" Poppy miaowed gleefully, as she went

even higher. "I'm really, really
good at climbing – OH!"
Suddenly, her paw slipped and
she almost lost her footing.

"Be careful, Poppy!" Barney
called anxiously.

Poppy stopped for a moment,
her heart beating fast. Then she
went on. The big branch was
getting very close now. One more

step, and—

"Look at me!" Poppy purred triumphantly. "I made it!"

"See, Henry?" Barney was jumping around excitedly at the bottom of the tree. "I told you she could do it!"

"She's still got to come down yet," Henry muttered, looking rather uncomfortable.

Coming down was a bit tricky too. But by now Poppy was so confident that there was no stopping her. She strolled from branch to branch, swung herself down onto the fence and then slid casually down the little tree.

"Well done, Poppy!" Barney said. "You were brilliant!"

"You're a really good climber,

Poppy," Lily added admiringly.

"Thanks." Poppy looked at Henry. "What do *you* think, Henry?" she mewed.

"OK, OK!" Henry miaowed reluctantly. "You're not bad for a pedigree cat."

"Come on, Pops." Barney swiped at Poppy's ear playfully. "Let's have a game of Hide-and-Seek!" And he dashed off towards the trees at the bottom of the garden. Lily and Henry followed.

Poppy stood there staring after them for a moment. She could hear Princess saying very clearly, *A pedigree cat* never *plays with common old moggies!*

"Oh, shut up, Princess!" Poppy miaowed loudly, and she

scampered off after her new friends.

While Poppy was playing in the garden, Lisa was on her way home from school. Her mum was at work today, so Lisa's gran had come to collect her.

"I can't wait to see Poppy again!" Mrs Kent said eagerly, as they walked home. "I'm so glad she's settled in well with you."

Lisa nodded. "Although I think she's having problems getting used to Barney!" she said, smiling.

"Well, Poppy *is* a pedigree kitten," Mrs Kent pointed out. She unlocked the Martins' front door. "Maybe Barney's a bit rough for her."

"Maybe," Lisa agreed doubtfully, as they went inside. "Poppy! Poppy, where are you?" she called.

But there was no sign of the kitten.

"She must have gone outside," Lisa said at last.

"Oh dear, I hope Poppy's all right in the garden on her own," Mrs Kent said anxiously, as they went outside. "She was always kept inside the run when she lived with me."

"Poppy?" Lisa called, looking round the garden.

Suddenly a white streak of fur shot out of the undergrowth at the bottom of the garden, with

Barney in hot pursuit.

"Hello, Lisa!" Poppy mewed chirpily. "Hello, Mrs Kent!" And that was all she had time to say before Barney jumped on her, and they both rolled over and over on the dusty path.

"*Poppy*!" Mrs Kent shrieked, horrified. "What's *happened* to you?"

Chapter Six

Poppy had never heard Mrs Kent shout before. She jumped to her paws in surprise. So did Barney. Henry and Lily, who were behind them, crept away into the long grass.

"What's the matter?" Poppy mewed. Why were Mrs Kent and

Lisa staring at her like that?

Then she looked down at herself. Her beautiful white coat was matted and covered with sticky grass seeds, and it was streaked with dirt and dust. Poppy could hardly believe what she'd done.

"Oh, Poppy!" Lisa's gran was so

shocked, she could hardly speak. "Your beautiful coat! It's ruined!"

Poppy hung her dusty little head. "I'm sorry, Lisa," she mewed. "I didn't mean to get all dirty. We were having so much fun, I didn't even notice. I'll never do it again!"

Barney gave her a nudge. "But, Poppy, we had loads of fun, and Henry and Lily really like you now!" he miaowed. "They're going to come round to play again tomorrow."

"They are?" Poppy brightened up a bit, but only for a minute. Then she was glum again. How could she have fun with her new friends, but still keep herself clean and beautiful for Lisa?

But when Poppy looked at her owner again, she couldn't believe her eyes. Lisa was *smiling*.

"Oh, Poppy!" Lisa laughed, scooping her kitten into her arms. "You look so funny! And cuter than ever!"

Funny? Cute? Poppy cheered up immediately. Lisa wasn't angry with her after all!

"But, Lisa, *look* at her coat!" Mrs Kent groaned.

"I don't care, Gran!" Lisa replied firmly, giving the kitten a hug. "I love Poppy *whatever* she looks like!"

"And I love you too, Lisa!" Poppy purred happily. She rubbed her head against Lisa's chin. All this time she'd been trying so hard to keep herself clean and beautiful. And Lisa didn't even *care*! Poppy felt very relieved indeed.

Lisa grinned as she carried her kitten into the house. "It looks like Poppy had fun playing with Barney," she said.

"Yes, I did," Poppy mewed. "But he cheats at Hide-and-Seek!"

"Ooh, I do not!" Barney yowled, as he bounded into the house behind them. Mrs Kent followed, still looking a bit worried.

Lisa fetched Poppy's brush and began to groom her coat. The kitten purred loudly as Barney helped out by giving her a few friendly licks too.

After ten minutes, Poppy's coat

was fluffy and white again. "I like being clean and beautiful," she miaowed to Barney. "But it's fun to get messy too!"

"Look, Gran." Lisa turned to Mrs Kent. "Poppy's coat is fine, really it is."

"Yes, I can see that," Mrs Kent admitted reluctantly.

"I'm starving!" Barney miaowed.

Poppy realised *she* was hungry too.

Both cats twined themselves around Lisa's legs as she opened a tin of catfood and spooned it into their bowls.

"Yum yum!" Poppy licked her lips, and began to tuck in.

Lisa's gran could hardly believe

her eyes. "I didn't think Poppy
would like tinned food," she said.

"Neither did I!" Poppy mewed.
"But I'm getting used to it. It's
really quite tasty – and you can
tell Princess I said so!"

"Do you want that?" Barney
asked. He'd finished his own
bowl, and was looking hungrily
at what was left in Poppy's.

"Yes, I do, greedy-guts!" Poppy replied, giving him a playful swipe with her paw.

"Well, Lisa, Poppy *does* seem very happy," Mrs Kent said, smiling. "I'm glad."

"I *love* it here," Poppy miaowed, then she yawned widely. "Time for a nap, I think."

"Lisa's bed, or the living room rug?" Barney asked.

Poppy thought for a moment. "Lisa's bed!" she replied. And the two cats galloped upstairs. They jumped onto Lisa's bed and curled up together in one tight, furry ball.

"This little house is really cosy," Poppy yawned, her eyelids already drooping. "There's lots of nice, warm places to curl up and have a snooze."

"I thought you said it was too small," Barney teased her, yawning himself.

"I was as snooty as Princess then!" Poppy replied sleepily. "But I'm not Poppy the Posh Kitten any more. From now on, I'm Poppy the *Pet* Kitten!"

Bob the Bouncy Kitten

To Lily – who also likes to leap up curtains!

Special thanks to Mary Hooper

Chapter One

"Got you, Bob!" yelled Amy
Myers, lifting her kitten from his
hiding place behind the ironing
board.

"At last!" sighed Amy's mum.
She picked up the cat basket and
opened the lid. "Come on, then,
Bob! It's for your own good," she
said.

For a good twenty minutes Amy and Mrs Myers had been chasing Bob, Amy's kitten, around the house. It was time for him to visit the vet's for his second flu injection. But Bob didn't want to be shut inside the basket. They'd chased him up and down the stairs, in and out of the bedrooms – all over the place!

"In you go, Bob," Amy said. She lowered the wriggling ginger bundle into the basket. Bob twitched and squirmed and made mewing noises of protest. "Shut the lid, Mum!"

From the basket, Bob looked up at them, his eyes dark and wide. Then, just as the lid was almost closed, he made a leap for

freedom. Squeezing himself out
of a tiny opening, he bounced
onto the carpet and raced across
the room.

"Oh, no!" Amy cried.

"The little devil!" said her mum,
annoyed. She put the basket
down. "I've got work to do,
Amy," she said. "I can't waste
any more time. I suggest you get

him in the basket and tell me when you've done it. Then I'll drive you to the vet's." She went upstairs to her office.

Amy sat on the floor and sighed. She could just see the point of Bob's ginger tail sticking out from under a cushion on the sofa. "You're a little horror," she said to him. She didn't mean it, though. Bob was gorgeous and she loved him to pieces. He had soft gingery fur with just a smudge of white under his chin and another on his squishy tummy. And he had soft pink paws – very soft, because he'd never been outside – and glinty green eyes. But Bob was also the friskiest, bounciest kitten she had ever seen!

Bob was Amy's first pet. She'd had him just four weeks and, because it was the summer holidays, she'd been with him nearly every moment of that time. She had photographs of him all over her bedroom wall, on the table next to her bed, and stuck inside her diary. And no prizes for guessing what the subject of her school summer project was . . .

Keeping an eye on the scrap of Bob's tail that she could see, Amy sat down on the floor and yawned. She'd been awake at five o' clock that morning. Bob had woken her up by bouncing onto the bed and licking her nose. When she hadn't said hello to him straight away, he'd gone down to the bottom of the bed and tunnelled under the duvet to play with her toes.

Amy had an idea. She stretched and yawned noisily, then curled up on the floor and pretended to go to sleep. But she kept one eye half open, to see what Bob would do.

After a couple of minutes, Bob came out from behind the cushion and made his way towards her, whiskers quivering, one dainty paw in front of the other.

Amy kept still as Bob stepped gently onto her leg. Then suddenly, in one swift movement, she scooped him up. "Got you!" she said to the surprised kitten.

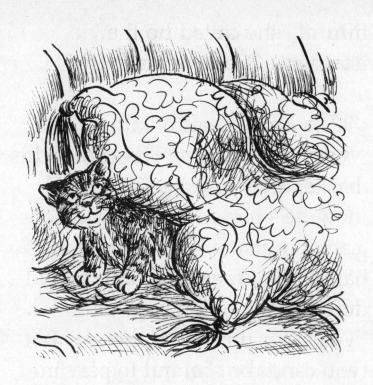

Quick as a flash, she plonked him inside the open basket and shut the lid.

Bob miaowed indignantly.

"Got you good and proper, this time," Amy said, smiling. She fastened the catch and carried the basket into the hall. "I've got him,

Mum!" she called up the stairway. "Can we go now?"

"He's a fine healthy kitten," the vet said, putting Bob back into his basket after his injection. "And now he's had his second jab he can go outside." She smiled at Amy. "Bob may be a bit groggy after this injection, so let him take it easy for the rest of the day. But you can take him out to play in the garden tomorrow."

Amy nodded happily. She could hardly wait. She and Bob were going to have such fun!

"That's good," Amy's mum said. "I hope that means Bob will be a bit quieter in the house, once he's had a run around outside. At the moment he races around like a whirlwind!"

"I expect he'll calm down a bit as he gets older," said the vet.

Amy and her mum left the surgery with Bob. Driving home, there wasn't a squeak or a miaow from the kitten. He just lay quietly at the bottom of his basket.

"I hope he's not feeling bad," Amy said anxiously.

When they reached home she carried the basket indoors, taking care not to bang it against anything. Still, everything was quiet in the basket.

"Do you think Bob's OK?" Amy asked her mum worriedly. "He didn't react like this after his first injection."

Mrs Myers shrugged. "Perhaps this one was stronger," she suggested.

Amy opened the lid of the basket, ready to lift her groggy kitten out. But as she did so, Bob shot out of the basket, so fast, he was a blur.

He leapt onto the arm of the sofa and bounced up to the window sill. "Fooled you!" he miaowed. Then he scampered up the curtains to sit on the curtain rail. He looked down at Amy and her mum, his green eyes shining.

"Feeling bad, did you say?" said Mrs Myers. "Gathering strength for his next big bounce, more like!"

Chapter Two

"Come along then, Bob," Amy said. "Time for you to meet the outside world!"

It was the following morning and Amy had hardly been able to sleep, with a lively Bob racing around her room for most of the night.

She opened the back door wide. "Look, Bob!" she went on. "Grass, trees and lots of different things to play with. You don't have to just sit indoors staring at everything now."

For the past four weeks Bob had often sat at the window, paws up against the glass, gazing out. Now he could actually get out there. Amy could hardly wait to see what he was going to do.

Bob was sitting on a kitchen chair, giving himself a wash. Seeing the open door, he bounced down and came to stand in the open doorway.

His nostrils twitched as he sniffed the fresh air. Then his ears quivered as they picked up outdoor noises that were new and strange to him.

He looked up at Amy, his green eyes big and wide. "Can I go out there, now?" he mewed.

"Don't be nervous, Bob," Amy said gently. "It's lovely outside. There's grass and bushes and a big tree and—"

"What are we waiting for, then?" Bob mewed loudly and, before Amy could say any more, he took off.

Amy ran after Bob as he bounded down the path, then plunged into the grass.

When he reached the end of the lawn and hit the cool earth of the flower bed, Bob stopped. "Wow!" he mewed. "This playground is just great!"

Bob bounced around the garden for some time, jumping at flies, playing hide and seek with Amy in the long grass and pouncing on things.

Suddenly, Bob spotted Georgina, Mrs-Neil-next-door's big grey cat. Georgina was

stretched out on the roof of her
owner's little garden shed, next to
the fence.

Bob ran over to the shed and
looked up at Georgina. Then he
looked back at Amy. "I'm going
up to make friends!" he miaowed.

"I wouldn't climb up there,
Bob," Amy warned. "Georgina is
a very grown-up cat. She might

not like bouncy kittens, and—"

But Bob didn't wait to hear the rest. Digging his claws into the rough wood of the fence, he scampered up then jumped onto the shed roof, next to Georgina.

The old grey cat opened one eye and looked lazily at the ball of ginger fluff that had suddenly appeared next to her.

Bob looked back at her. "Hello," he mewed. "I live in the house next door."

Georgina just kept on looking at him with one eye.

"Anyway," Bob went on, "do you fancy a game of 'pounce the mouse'?" He jumped back and forth to demonstrate.

Georgina opened her other eye.

Her tail began to swish from side to side. "Watch it, or I'll pounce on you," she miaowed, sounding a little annoyed.

"I think you'd better come down, Bob," Amy called, seeing that the old cat was looking angry. "I don't think Georgina likes kittens."

But Bob didn't listen. "Oh, go on!" he mewed to Georgina. "It'll be fun!" To get her in the mood, he bounced right up to Georgina and pounced on her swaying tail.

Hissing loudly, Georgina sprang to her feet, ears flattened and fur bristling. Suddenly she seemed twice her size.

Chapter Three

Bob shrank back, startled.
"Sorry," he mewed weakly.
"Didn't mean to offend you." He
waited a moment, then crept
closer again. "Perhaps another
time . . ."

Georgina began to make a
funny growling sound in the back

of her throat. But *still* Bob didn't take the hint. She gave him a side-swipe with her paw. "Go away!" she hissed.

"Bob!" Amy called. "Come down *now*! Georgina doesn't want to play."

Just then, Mrs Neil came out

into her garden to hang out her washing. "You've got your new kitten out here!" she said, putting down the basket. "Oh, isn't he gorgeous?"

Amy nodded proudly. "It's his first day in the big world. He's just introduced himself to your Georgina, but I don't think she was too keen. She gave him a clip round the ear."

Mrs Neil grinned. "Georgina is an old lady now, like me. She likes to keep naughty little boys like Bob in check." Mrs Neil put down her washing basket and said, "Can I lift the little tyke down for a cuddle?"

Amy smiled. "Course you can." Watched by a disapproving

Georgina, Mrs Neil reached up and lifted Bob from the shed roof. "He's a darling!" she said, stroking Bob and tickling him under the chin.

Bob wriggled out of Mrs Neil's arms and ran onto her shoulders to settle himself round the back of her neck. Mrs Neil laughed. "Oh, they're lovely when they're this young," she said. "I sometimes wish they could stay this small and cute for ever."

"They're so naughty, though," Amy said, and she told Mrs Neil some of the things that Bob had got up to, like hanging on the curtains, and drinking the bath water, and licking butter out of the dish. "And half of those my

mum doesn't even know about!"
she finished.

Mrs Neil nodded. "Yes, now
you come to mention it, I
remember Georgina doing the
same. Maybe it's as well that they
do grow up, then," she said.

Bob decided he was bored with
all this chat. He took a flying leap

from Mrs Neil's shoulders and landed on a fence post. Then he dropped back into his own garden. They watched him springing like a hare over the lawn.

"Off he goes," Mrs Neil said. "He's a right little tearaway!"

Bob ran right down to the bottom of the garden and, without hesitating, shinned straight up the big oak tree in the corner.

"They love climbing trees," Mrs Neil said. "And it's good for their claws, too. It sharpens them, you know."

"It's a huge tree, though," Amy said, frowning worriedly. "I hope he doesn't get stuck up there."

They watched as Bob rounded the trunk of the tree and began to skitter and scratch his way out onto a branch.

"Kittens are quite clever," Mrs Neil said. "They don't usually go anywhere they can't get down from."

Just as she said that, they saw Bob stop and look all around him. He began to miaow loudly.

"Oh! He's stuck!" Amy said. "I knew it!" She ran over to the tree.

Bob stared down at her. "This is soooo exciting," he called. "I can see into all the other gardens from here!"

"What if he really can't get down?" Amy cried.

Mrs Neil tutted anxiously,

watching Bob. Then she said, "I've got an idea. It used to work with Georgina when she wouldn't come in . . ." She went into her house and reappeared a few minutes later with a box of cat biscuits.

"I'm going to stay up here for ever!" Bob miaowed.

"He hasn't moved at all," Amy said. "I think he's scared of falling off."

"Let's see if this works," said Mrs Neil, pushing open her garden gate. She strode into Amy's garden, shaking the box of cat biscuits.

Bob recognised the sound. Food!

Mrs Neil shook again. "Here, puss-puss-puss!" she said.

"Purreoww!" Georgina, on hearing the familiar noise, had jumped down from the shed and was sitting at Mrs Neil's feet, looking expectantly up at the box.

"Yes, there's some for you as well," Mrs Neil said, and she bent and poured out a few biscuits for Georgina.

"Shake it again, Mrs Neil," Amy said. "Bob heard you shaking it, too!"

As the box was shaken again, Bob changed his mind about staying up the tree for ever. His tummy was rumbling. Much as he liked climbing trees, he decided that he liked biscuits better.

Carefully, he managed to turn on the branch. "Phew! That was

a bit tricky!" he mewed.

"He's coming down! Hurrah!" said Amy, as Bob edged back to the main trunk of the tree then scampered down it. "I thought I was going to have to get the fire brigade out," she told Bob as he crunched on his biscuits.

"Let's hope he's learned not to go where he shouldn't," Mrs Neil said, smiling.

"Yes, Bob," Amy agreed. "No more climbing dangerous trees, OK?"

Bob didn't seem to hear her. And as soon as he'd finished off his biscuits, he took off again like a small ginger rocket, racing up the garden and into the kitchen.

Amy stayed talking to Mrs Neil

for a while, stroking Georgina, who seemed in a much better mood now the cheeky young kitten had gone away.

Suddenly there was a short scream from inside. "Amy!" Mrs Myers shouted. "Come and get your kitten out of this mixing bowl *immediately*!"

"Oops," said Amy.

"Maybe he hasn't *quite* learned his lesson," said Mrs Neil.

Chapter Four

Two days later, Amy stood at the
foot of the big oak tree, staring
up. "Not again, Bob!" she said.
Through the leaves and branches
she could just see a trace of
gingery fur. It was only a
glimpse, though, because Bob
was a long way up.

"Come on, Bob!" she called. "Puss-puss-puss!"

Through the greenery came a faint miaow. "Not just yet, Amy . . ."

"Bob-Bob-Bob!" Amy called. "Come on down, boy!"

The miaow was a little louder this time. "Not just *yet*, Amy. I'm busy!"

Amy sighed, worriedly. Bob seemed to be stuck again. He had been going into the garden for three days now, but instead of the big outdoors using up his energy, it seemed to make him bouncier than ever. He was still always getting into mischief.

She went back inside the house and brought out a box of cat biscuits. "Bob-Bob-Bob!" she called. "Lovely rabbit-flavoured biscuits!" She shook the box like mad.

Bob stopped examining the old empty bird's nest he'd found on one of the branches. *Mmm, I could do with a snack*, he thought. It had been quite a hectic morning. "Coming!" he miaowed.

He made his way back down the tree, arriving with a scrabble and a bounce at the bottom.

"Oh, thank goodness!" Amy tipped some biscuits onto the ground. "Bob, I do wish you wouldn't keep climbing trees. I'm always frightened you won't be able to get back down."

Insulted, Bob pretended not to hear that. *I could get down from any tree*, he thought huffily.

The very next day, Bob was in disgrace. Mrs Myers had been making cheese sandwiches for lunch. Bob had decided that he fancied a bit of cheese sandwich too. He'd bounced onto the kitchen table to help himself.

Luckily, Amy's mum had been looking in the fridge at the time. Amy had put Bob back on the floor straight away.

But Bob wasn't put off so easily. He'd bounced onto the table again, and this time Mrs Myers had seen Bob up there herself. Now he was in big trouble.

Amy sat picking miserably at her sandwich. Bob was outside, miaowing away and scratching at the back door. "Can Bob come in again now?" Amy asked.

"No," Mrs Myers said. "He's got to learn his lesson."

Just then, two gingery-white tufty ears appeared in the glass panel of the back door. "Oh, look!" Amy cried. "Bob's

standing on his hind legs to try to
look in. Oh, Mum, isn't he sweet?"

"Sweet – and very naughty," her
mum said. But Amy could see she
was smiling a little.

Amy took the dirty plates to the
sink. "Can I go out to him,
please?"

Her mum nodded, then said, "I suppose I'll have to eat all the banana custard myself . . ."

Amy loved banana custard. "Well . . . I'm sure Bob will be OK on his own for just a little bit longer."

Chapter Five

Bob's cute pose at the back door
hadn't worked. Mrs Myers *still*
hadn't let him come back in.

He looked around for
something to cheer him up . . .
The oak tree! He miaowed one
last time at the back door, then
raced across the lawn.

In seconds he was bouncing from one large, leafy branch to another, chasing after sparrows. But they soon all flew away.

Bob swatted some tiny insects that were scurrying along the branch. He loved it up here. The branch swayed up and down as a light breeze ruffled its leaves.

The kitten looked around him. He could see for miles! He could see that snobby cat Georgina on the patio next door. And a black tom-cat peering over the garden wall two doors down.

And then Bob saw something else. Something quite frightening. "Oh, dear!" he mewed. "I need to get help!"

Amy scraped her pudding bowl clean. Bob had stopped scratching at the door.

She went out into the garden to find him, but she couldn't see him anywhere. Frowning, she went right down to the bushes at the bottom, calling as she went, but she still couldn't see him. She searched in the shed, but he wasn't there, either.

There was no sign of Bob anywhere. Unless . . . Amy walked over to the foot of the old oak tree and looked up. "Bob?" she called.

Faintly, from far up in the tree, she heard an answering miaow.

"Oh, not again!" Sighing, she trudged back indoors to get the box of cat biscuits.

"Bob-Bob-Bob!" Amy called a few seconds later. She rattled the biscuit box hard. "Come on, boy! Lovely biscuits!"

Amy called and called, and shook and shook. The miaowing continued. And to Amy, it seemed to get louder and louder. But there was no rustle from the leaves to tell her that Bob was making his way down.

"You must *really* be stuck this time, Bob," Amy muttered worriedly. She went indoors to see if her mum would call the fire brigade.

Mrs Myers was upstairs in the spare room, working at her computer. "Don't be silly!" she said, when Amy told her the story. "You can't expect the fire brigade to come out just because a kitten's been up a tree for a few minutes."

"It's not just a few minutes," Amy said. "It's nearly half an hour now. Suppose he falls?"

Mrs Myers shook her head. "Left to their own devices, kittens will always come down trees by themselves," she said. "You've just got to leave him to it. Do something else and forget about him for a while!"

She pressed a key and her printer started to whirr. "I really must get on, Amy. That kitten gets quite enough attention from you without me fussing round him. He'll come down when he's good and ready."

Amy sighed. She went downstairs and out to the oak tree. Half-heartedly, she rattled the biscuit box and called Bob once more, but with no luck. Bob's miaowing was becoming quite frantic now. Amy was sure he was scared to bits.

Suddenly Amy's eyes fell on the old wooden ladder that was propped up against the wall at the bottom of the garden . . .

She went over to the ladder and tried to pull it away from the wall. It was very heavy. Amy heaved again, holding the highest rungs she could reach.

Slowly, the top of the ladder came away from the wall. With all her strength, she dragged it towards the oak tree and let go. Amy held her breath.

Yes! The ladder landed with a clatter against the thick trunk. Pleased with herself, Amy pushed it firmly into position. It seemed safe and secure.

"I'm coming, Bob!" she called,

putting a foot on the first rung.

There was an answering miaow. "Hurry, Amy!" Bob called.

As she climbed higher, Amy could see a tiny gingery face looking down at her through the branches. The ladder wobbled slightly and she stopped and held onto a branch. It was a bit scary. She didn't want to look down.

Bob gave another long, drawn-out mi-aooow! "Come up and see what I can see!"

"Yes, I know you're scared," Amy said. "I am too. But I'm coming for you now." Glancing over into Mrs Neil's garden, she saw Georgina pacing up and down outside Mrs Neil's greenhouse. *That's odd*, Amy

thought. She climbed up another two rungs of the ladder.

Bob watched her intently, his green eyes alert. "Look again, Amy!" he mewed.

And then Amy's eyes opened wide. She could see Mrs Neil lying on the greenhouse floor. "Mrs Neil!" she cried. "Are you all right, Mrs Neil?"

There was no reply. Amy gasped and leaned over to get a better look. Mrs Neil was very still. What on earth was wrong? Was she really badly hurt?

Amy began to feel frightened. "Mrs Neil!" she called again. "Oh, Mrs Neil!"

"That's what I wanted to show you!" miaowed Bob from further up the tree.

Amy glanced up. "You'll have to wait, Bob," she said. "I've got to tell Mum!" And she scrambled down the ladder as quickly as she could.

Chapter Six

"Mum! Mum! Come quickly!" Amy shouted, running up the stairs two at a time. "Mum!"

As Amy burst through the door of Mrs Myer's office, she saw her mum was on the phone.

"Excuse me one moment," Mrs Myers said very politely into the phone. Then she put her hand over the receiver and turned to Amy. "What is it, Amy?" she asked in a rather cross voice.

"You've got to come down, Mum!" Amy cried.

Mrs Myers sighed. "It's not that kitten again, is it? What's he done now?"

Amy shook her head. "It's not Bob," she said, hopping about from foot to foot. "It's Mrs Neil! She's out in her greenhouse and she's fallen on the floor . . . Her leg's all funny – and she's not moving or talking to me!"

Mrs Myers stood up quickly and spoke into the receiver. "I'm so sorry, it's a domestic emergency. May I ring you back?" She put the phone down. "Let's go!"

Mrs Myers followed Amy back down the stairs. "But how on earth did you come to see Mrs Neil in her greenhouse?" she asked as they ran.

"I was . . . er . . . climbing the ladder," Amy said.

"Well, really, Amy! You know you shouldn't have done that without asking!" her mum said.

"I had to!" Amy pleaded. "Bob was really and truly stuck. I mean, he still is!"

"Well and truly stuck, eh?" repeated her mum as they ran through the kitchen. "Who's that, then?"

There in the kitchen, nose in his bowl and crunching cat biscuits for all he was worth, was Bob.

"Oh!" Amy cried.

As her mum disappeared out of the kitchen door, Amy swooped on Bob, picked him up and hugged him. "You got down on your own again, you pest of a kitten!"

"Of course I did!" Bob purred. "Don't I always?"

Carrying Bob, Amy ran out into the garden. Her mum called over the fence and told her to dial 999 and ask for an ambulance to come straight away.

Still holding Bob tightly, Amy turned and ran back into the house. Oh, she hoped Mrs Neil would be all right!

*

Twenty minutes later, the ambulance had arrived.

"I had a dizzy turn," Mrs Neil told the ambulance crew. "I don't remember anything else until I heard the ambulance siren outside . . ."

Mrs Neil was weak and shaken up after her fall. She had to go to hospital to have X-rays taken of her injured leg, to see if it was broken.

Bob sat perfectly still in Amy's arms, watching as Mrs Neil was lifted onto a stretcher.

Mrs Neil beckoned Amy over to her. "Thank you so much, my dear," she said in a very faint voice. "I don't know how long I'd have been lying here if you hadn't seen me . . ."

"That's OK," Amy said shyly.

"I helped too!" purred Bob. But no one seemed to notice.

"Yes, you did well, love," the ambulance woman said to Amy, placing a soft red blanket round Mrs Neil. "It was a good job you were up that ladder."

Amy's mum nodded. "But you

really mustn't use that ladder on your own again, young lady," she added sternly. Then she smiled and gave Amy a quick hug.

Bob miaowed loudly. "What about me?"

Holding Bob with one arm, Amy hugged her mum back. Then she looked down at her kitten. "We ought to thank Bob, really," she said.

"Who's Bob?" asked the ambulance woman. "Your brother?"

"No, this is Bob," Amy said, holding up her kitten. "If he hadn't got stuck up the oak tree, I would never have climbed the ladder and seen Mrs Neil lying on the floor."

Bob gave a purry miaow. "It wasn't *quite* like that, Amy. I *wasn't* stuck!"

"Then I'm very grateful to Bob, too!" Mrs Neil said shakily as the ambulance crew carried her over to the ambulance. "I might have been on that floor all night – and who knows what might have become of me! When I get back I shall buy Bob a big bag of cat treats to say thank you."

Bob sat in Amy's arms and purred. They'd got it slightly wrong, but at least everyone knew now that he'd had a part in the rescue. And a big bag of cat treats sounded pretty good to him!

Just as Mrs Neil was being lifted

into the ambulance, Bob wriggled out of Amy's arms. He leapt onto the hedge to have a good look round.

"I'm watching you, Bob!" Amy called to him warningly.

Bob pretended not to hear. "Bye, Mrs Neil!" he miaowed. "Hope you're all right! You don't mind if I give your apple tree a try, do you?" Then he bounded down onto the lawn – and found himself face to face with Georgina.

Bob bounced back a few paces in alarm. Last time he'd been this close to Georgina, she'd given him a nasty swipe.

But this time she was purring, so he plonked himself down next to her and started to purr too. "Feel free! Anyone who rescues my Mrs Neil is a friend of mine. And though I'm a bit old to do much climbing myself now, I can recommend the lilac tree and the pear tree, too."

"Right! Thanks!" squeaked Bob,

hardly able to believe his luck. In a blur of ginger fur, he zipped across the lawn and shinned straight up the apple tree.

"Oh, good heavens!" said Mrs Neil, who had seen Bob through the open ambulance doors. "There he goes again!" Apples fell to the floor as Bob scampered to the top of the tree.

"Time for another rescue?" said the ambulance woman, smiling.

Amy shook her head. "Now I *know* Bob can get down by himself." Then she frowned and turned to Mrs Neil. "But if Bob wasn't stuck up the oak tree, Mrs Neil, why didn't he come down for biscuits like he usually does?"

Mrs Neil shook her head. "Very

unusual," she said.

Amy smiled. "I think he saw that you had fallen and wanted me to climb up and see you, too."

Everyone laughed.

"That's a good one!" said the ambulance man.

"Don't be silly, love!" said Amy's mum.

"It's a nice thought, though," said Mrs Neil.

Bob miaowed happily as he swayed in the branches at the top of the apple tree.

Mrs Neil's leg was very sore from her fall, but luckily it wasn't broken. A few days later, the ambulance brought her home again. Apart from some nasty

bruises, the old lady seemed fine.
But from then on, Bob always
kept an eye on her – whenever he
was bouncing up trees . . .